Please return

You may

You can re

Withdrawn

____

30/61

First published in the UK in 2020
by New Frontier Publishing Europe Ltd.
Uncommon, 126 New King's Road, London, SW6 4LZ
www.newfrontierpublishing.co.uk

ISBN: 978-1-912858-34-7

A CIP catalogue record for this book
is available from the British Library.

Edited by Stephanie Stahl
Designed by Verity Clark

Printed and bound in China
1 3 5 7 9 10 8 6 4 2

Bear
was
THERE

For Dad.
– S A G

A big thanks to everyone in the Collaborate Agency for their input and hard work.

Thank you also to all the team at New Frontier Publishing. A special thanks to Stephanie Stahl, an extremely insightful and thoughtful editor, and to Verity Clark for all her amazing design talent and expertise.

Sally Anne Garland

Bear was THERE

Sally Anne Garland

NEW FRONTIER PUBLISHING

LOVE.

The first thing Mouse felt was love, as he lay in the warmth of his mother's fur inside a cosy nook of a tree.

As he grew, Mouse felt
curious to play outside.

'Be careful,' his mother whispered.
'There is DANGER. Bear is out there.'

Mouse was a little nervous,
but timidly crept out.

Outside, he smelt the fresh air and gazed in wonder at the world around him. A light breeze was running through his whiskers. Mouse felt **excited**.

But in the distance, he spotted a **big dark** shadow.

'Quick!' his mother warned. 'It must be Bear,' so they scampered away.

Eventually, Mouse adventured into the long, tall grass of a big meadow.

Flowers, bugs and insects danced in the sun's warmth.

He ran across the field; his heart was beating fast.

Mouse felt HAPPY.

Mouse came to a clear stream. For the first time, he saw water and beautiful, shiny fish swimming about.

Mouse felt **amazed**,

however his mother called to him in the distance,
'Careful, Little Mouse. Bear could be close.'

So he did not stay.

Soon Mouse grew bigger and bigger, and it was time for him to leave his mother's home to build his very own.

He journeyed further into the wood and settled in a safe, towering tree. He happily scampered and scurried around until one day...

Mouse was playing in the soft grass
when he heard the dry snap of a
branch behind him.

Someone was there.

Mouse darted behind some leaves.

A **huge**, familiar shadow, a lot bigger and a lot
scarier than before, was standing still over him.

It
was
Bear.

Trembling, Mouse looked up as Bear gazed down. The woods were silent. Mouse was surprised at how kind Bear's eyes seemed.

Then with a sniff and a soft rustle of leaves, Bear gently padded away.

Maybe Bear isn't so scary after all, thought Mouse.

Time passed.

Mouse watched the wind play with the fallen brown leaves. His neighbours moved away and Mouse felt alone. The air became a frosty quiet.

Mouse shivered as the ground
grew cold and hard beneath him.

Then winter came.

Mouse was woken up by an icy
wind. It was roaring through
the trees. Branches crashed and
the wood was dangerous.

Mouse felt afraid.

He scrambled away, straight
into the raging storm.

Mouse looked lost and shivery whilst struggling through the snow. Suddenly, Bear was THERE, but Mouse did not feel scared. Instead, he felt a strange relief, for he knew Bear was surely heading towards a shelter.

Mouse began to follow him.

Through the frosty gales and biting cold, Little Mouse kept walking. Ahead, Bear's shadowy hulk lumbered on.

Then Bear disappeared into the opening of a cave . . .

With the last strength he had left,
Mouse followed.

As he struggled inside, he found
Bear curled up, almost asleep, on
the cave's dry floor.

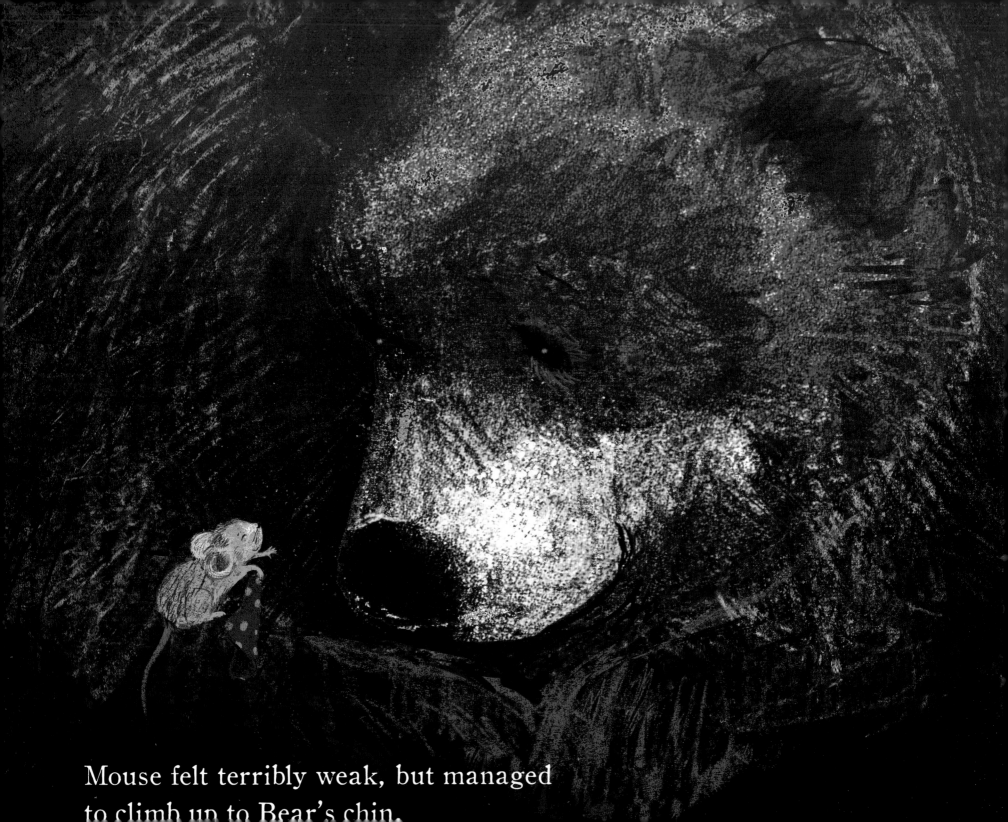

Mouse felt terribly weak, but managed
to climb up to Bear's chin.

Nestling into the warmth of Bear's thick fur, he was no longer alone or afraid.

Mouse felt **safe** and peaceful.

Bear gently placed his paw onto Mouse's little head.

Bear was there and Mouse felt . . .

LOVED.